Weekly Reader Presents

Danger: Boober Cooking

(Original Title: Boober Fraggle's Celery Soufflé)

By Louise Gikow   Pictures by Kelly Oechsli

Muppet Press

Henry Holt and Company

NEW YORK

Published by Henry Holt and Company,
521 Fifth Avenue, New York, New York 10175

Library of Congress Cataloging in Publication Data
Gikow, Louise.
Boober Fraggle's celery soufflé.
Summary: Boober Fraggle shares his favorite recipe for
celery soufflé.
[1. Puppets—Fiction.   2. Cookery—Fiction.   3. Stories
in rhyme]   I. Oechsli, Kelly, ill.   II. Title.
PZ8.3.G376Bo   1984   [E]   84-6858
ISBN: 0-03-000722-4

Printed in the United States of America

ISBN 0-03-000722-4

This book is a presentation of
Weekly Reader Books

Weekly Reader Books offers book clubs for children
from preschool through high school.

For further information write to:
Weekly Reader Books
4343 Equity Drive
Columbus, Ohio 43228

Danger:
Boober Cooking

BOOBER is a Fraggle
And he lives in Fraggle Rock,
Which is underneath, or right behind,
A workshop owned by Doc.
The Fraggles down in Fraggle Rock
Are happy as can be
Except for Boober Fraggle,
As you very soon will see.

Fraggles come in many colors,
Just like lollipops or gum,
And their fur is soft and fuzzy,
And they like to sing and hum,

And they also like to dance and play
And swim and things like that.
That is, except for Boober.

Boober likes to wear a hat.

And underneath his hat,
He sighs and worries all the day.
He's much too superstitious
To make any time for play.

His job is doing laundry,
Which is mostly his own socks,
And he scrubs them and he rubs them
And he beats them on the rocks.

The only other thing
He ever really likes to do
Is cooking up a pie or cake
Or roast or hash or stew.
His talents in the kitchen
Are renowned both far and wide,

And what he does
with radishes
Is not to be denied.

Boober's favorite recipe
Is Celery Soufflé.
He loves it so that if he could,
He'd make it every day.

And just in case you want a taste,
I asked him if he could
Explain just how he makes it.
And Boober said he would!

So here is Boober's recipe
For Celery Soufflé.
It's really very simple,
And it all starts out this way:

"First you need some celery,"
Says Boober. "That is clear.
Despite the risks you take
When picking celery down here.
The Garden of the Gorgs is where
All the celery grows,
And it is really scary there,
As any Fraggle knows!

"The Gorgs are all quite fearsome—
They're as giant as can be.
They're twenty million times the size
Of either you or me!
(Well, actually they're not.
But they are big enough to fear
And they try to stomp on Fraggles
When they see us coming near.)

"Then once you've risked your life and limb,
And celery you've got
The next thing that you need to find
Is just the right-sized pot.

Though usually I never do.
I seem to be unlucky.
The other Fraggles use my pots
And leave them kind of yucky.

"The next of the ingredients is water—
Just one spoon.
You get it from the pond
In the Great Hall on any afternoon.

That is, if they don't splash you
And you come down with a cold
And you end up with the sniffles
While your celery grows mold!

"Another thing you need
To give it flavor is a bit
Of limpet leaf, which grows quite wild
Down in the Smelly Pit.

The Pit will surely make you ill—
Its odor has no charm.
And then, while climbing down it,
You just might break your arm!

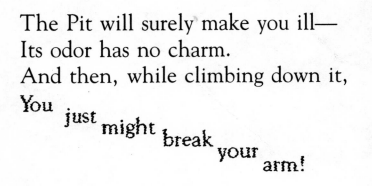

"With limpet leaf for flavoring,
There's one more thing you need:
You need a pinch of wompus root—
Or else some wompus seed.

But wompus roots can trip you.
You might fall on your nose,
And break a leg or scrape your knee—
Or maybe both of those!

"Then mix it all together
In the pot of the wrong size,
And cook it very carefully,
Away from bugs and flies.

And when it's done, be quiet,
Or you're sure to make it fall
And you'll wish you hadn't asked me
How to cook soufflé at all!

"And come to think of it,
I wish you hadn't asked me how,
For I was getting hungry,
And I thought I'd cook one now.
Such awful things can happen
Before you can be fed,

"I think that I will stay right here
And spend the day in bed!"